The Monster War

Written by Robert Hood

Illustrated by Chris Lynch

sundance™

 **sundance**™

 a black dog book

Published by
Sundance Publishing, LLC
33 Boston Post Road West
Suite 440
Marlborough, MA 01752
1-800-343-8204
www.sundancepub.com

Copyright © text Robert Hood
Copyright © illustrations Chris Lynch

First published 2002 by
Pearson Education Australia Pty. Limited
95 Coventry Street
South Melbourne 3205 Australia
Exclusive United States Distribution: Sundance Publishing

Guided Reading Level K
Guided reading levels assigned by Sundance Publishing using the text characteristics
described by Fountas & Pinnell in their book *Guided Reading*, published by Heinemann.

ISBN 978-0-7608-6710-5

Printed by Nordica International Ltd.
Manufactured in Guangzhou, China
April, 2010
Nordica Job#: 04-23-10
Sundance/Newbridge PO#: 225906

Contents

Characters

Stu wants to be liked at his new school.

Sean loves to collect monster models.

Alice likes making friends at school.

Chapter One
A Problem

The class stared at Stu, the new kid. He was talking on and on about monsters.

"In fact, monsters are called 'daikaiju' in Japan," Stu went on hurriedly. "But they're really just guys in rubber suits. When I lived in Japan, I used to hang out on the monster movie sets. I even watched the movie *Titanoid Versus the Pulsatron* being filmed."

Some of the kids started to look impressed. *Titanoid Versus the Pulsatron* was the most popular movie in town. In it, the famous giant reptile Titanoid battled with a huge, pulsating beast from outer space. The film had just opened, and everyone wanted to see it.

One of the kids in class, Sean, was a big monster fan. "Do you expect us to believe you had something to do with the Titanoid movies?" Sean asked Stu.

Stu gulped. Why did he always get carried away, saying things like that to try to impress people? He had never watched a monster movie being filmed. So why did he say he had?

Stu felt that he had to be really different or interesting for the other kids to accept him. As the new kid at school, he thought that if he told fantastic stories, the other kids would like him. Then they might even become his friends.

"My Uncle Jake worked for Ishiro Kurosawa, the director of the Titanoid movies," Stu explained. "Uncle Jake was a cameraman. He became close friends with Kurosawa. It was pretty exciting to be on the movie set."

Of course the kids wanted to know more, so Stu began making up things. He could tell that Sean didn't really believe him. But luckily Miss Pender, their teacher, walked into the classroom before Sean could ask Stu any tricky questions.

Miss Pender made an announcement to the class. "Many of you like to collect certain objects as your hobby," she said. "I know that Sean, Kelly, and Phoebe all have collections. And Stu, you have a special collection of monsters, I believe?"

"I bet mine's much better!" exclaimed Sean proudly.

"It doesn't matter whose is better, Sean," said Miss Pender. "What's important is that you all enjoy your hobbies. So I suggest that next week we have a Collectors' Fair. You can all share what you collect with the class."

Everyone was very excited. But Stu was worried, and he thought about the fair for the rest of the day.

After school, Sean stopped at Stu's locker. Stu started stuffing books into his backpack and tried to ignore Sean. But it didn't work.

"You can't fool me with your stories," Sean said. "And my guess is that you don't even have a great collection. I think you're making it all up!"

"Mine's fantastic!" said Stu defensively. "It's the best!" But Stu looked worried, and Sean gave him a knowing look.

"So, do you really have monster stuff that you got in Japan from the movie sets?" Sean asked Stu.

"Oh yes!" replied Stu firmly.

"Then why don't you bring your director friend along, too?" Sean asked.

Stu's face paled. He suddenly realized what he'd been saying.

Stu had a pretty good collection of monster stuff, though it wasn't that great. He had grown up in Tokyo. His father had worked there for ten years. But nothing else he'd said was true.

"Well, I still don't believe you," Sean said. "But we'll see at the fair who has the best collection. We'll have our own Monster War!"

All of the kids who had gathered around Stu and Sean in the hallway cheered. Suddenly Stu didn't feel very well.

Chapter Two

A Solution

Stu really was in hot water. Without any special monster model in his collection, everyone would think he was boring. They would know that he had lied, and they would not want to be his friends.

"What's new, Stu?" asked a cheery voice. It was Alice. She had black hair and a big smile.

"Nothing," Stu muttered.

"You look like the world's about to end. What's the problem?" Alice asked.

"It's my uncle's friend, the director," Stu said. "I can't bring him to school like Sean asked. He lives in Japan."

Alice shrugged. "No one expects you to do that."

"This Titanoid thing is just a fad anyway," said Alice. "Very few kids would know who Ishiro Kurosawa is, and no one would have a clue about what he looks like." Alice walked along with Stu and kept chatting away with him. Stu was happy to have the company.

Stu thought he'd never solve his problem. But by the time he and Alice reached his street, he had a plan. It had come from something Alice had said. Stu waved goodbye to Alice and rushed inside his house. He had to get busy putting his plan into action.

Stu headed for the phone and quickly
dialed a familiar phone number.

"Hello, Uncle Jake?" Stu said as soon as
his uncle answered. Uncle Jake was at
work, but Stu couldn't wait to talk with
him. "Can you please do me a favor?"
Stu asked quickly.

"Slow down," his uncle said. "Now what's all of this about?"

"This is urgent. I need you to save my life," said Stu.

"Save your life?" Uncle Jake chuckled. "Sounds to me like you're looking for Superman. He's out at the moment." His uncle laughed at his own joke.

"You've got to help me, Uncle Jake. Otherwise I'm doomed," Stu said sadly.

"Hmmm, it does sound serious," said his uncle. "What do I have to do?"

"Ask Taro to pretend to be a famous film director," Stu declared. Taro was a Japanese man who worked in his uncle's bakery. Stu carefully explained his problem to his uncle and the solution that he'd come up with.

If no one knew what Ishiro Kurosawa looked like, then he could just as easily look like Taro. Stu thought it was a good plan, except Uncle Jake wouldn't agree to it.

"Don't be silly, Stuart," he said. "You can't expect Taro to lie. Making up stories won't help you fit in at school. It'll only make matters worse."

"But Uncle Jake . . ."

"Work out your problems honestly, Stu," Uncle Jake said sternly.

Work out his problems honestly? How could Stu do that without looking like a complete loser?

On Saturday morning, Stu wandered around trying to think of a plan. Suddenly, he saw what looked like a large dinosaur on the top of a building. What was it?

As he got closer, he saw that it was an inflated rubber dinosaur, maybe twelve feet tall. It was tied to the top of a building in a used car lot.

The dinosaur was part of a "Monster Sale" promotion at LeBon Motors. The T-Rex dinosaur was huge and ugly, but it was very cool. If Stu had a monster that size in his collection, he would definitely win the Monster War! Then Stu remembered that Alice's father owned LeBon Motors. Now he had another plan!

Chapter Three

The Fair

On Monday, the day of the Collectors' Fair, the weather was sunny. Miss Pender arranged tables outside, and the students spread out their collections. There were baseball cards, dolls, model trains, comics, stamps, and even marbles.

But it was Sean's table that attracted the most attention. His table was covered with monsters.

Some of the models were small and plain. Others were very complex and special enough to win any Monster War. And right in the middle of his collection, Sean had displayed the latest Titanoid Action Figure. It was more than three feet tall and looked very cool.

Nearby, Stu's table was looking a bit bare. He'd only been able to find half a dozen interesting models. Most of Stu's collection looked very ordinary beside Sean's. Some kids complimented Stu on his collection, but it was clear that they thought Sean's was better.

"Wait until you see my best piece," Stu said to Sean. "It's huge!"

"Where's it hidden?" asked Sean.

"It's on the way!" replied Stu, trying to act cool.

Suddenly someone shouted, and everyone went to look. A large shadow fell across the playground. Alice appeared, dragging a squeaky wagon.

On the wagon was the inflatable T-Rex from LeBon Motors. Everyone gasped.

"See!" yelled Stu. "I asked Alice to drag it in as a surprise. It's the biggest thing in my collection. Isn't it fantastic?"

The other kids barely heard what Stu said. A gust of wind came up and whipped his words away. It also grabbed the T-Rex.

The rubber monster lifted up into the air, dragging Alice with it. She clung to the rope, yelling for help. Stu rushed over and grabbed the rope. He held on tightly. But the wind blew harder, and they couldn't hold T-Rex down by themselves.

Stu felt his feet scraping over the ground as T-Rex flew across the playground. If he and Alice let go, T-Rex would fly away. But if they didn't let T-Rex go, they'd both be pulled into the road next to the school! Then Sean grabbed the rope, too. The three of them stopped T-Rex and pulled it back toward the fair. Sean tied one of the ropes firmly to a large bench.

Chapter Four

The Truce

By now everyone was laughing and shouting. Sean slapped Stu on the back. "That was terrific!"

"Yeah," agreed Stu, "it was neat!"

"And that's a very cool monster," Sean added. "I'd love to have something like that in my collection."

Then Allen, one of the other kids in class, shouted, "Hey, I've seen that T-Rex before!"

Uh oh! Stu held his breath.

"It was at the used car lot where my mom was buying a car," Allen continued.

"Wait a minute, Stu!" Alice said. "You didn't tell me you were going to say this T-Rex was from *your* collection."

Stu looked at Alice and then at Sean. Now Stu would have to admit the truth.

"It's not really mine," Stu said quietly. "Alice's dad owns it. I just thought it would be a . . ." Stu hesitated. Then he finally said, "I thought it would be a good joke."

Sean didn't look as if he thought it was a good joke. He walked stiffly up to Stu.

"You were just trying to win the Monster War, weren't you?" Sean said angrily to Stu. "You even said that the T-Rex was part of your collection."

Stu felt embarrassed. He looked at his sneakers. "Sorry," he said. "It's hard being the new kid. I guess that's why I told those stories. I was just trying to fit in."

Sean scowled at Stu, ignoring his last comment. "I knew you were lying all along. All of that stuff about your uncle knowing a famous monster movie director is a lie, too, isn't it?"

Stu noticed that Miss Pender and lots of the other kids were watching him. He wanted to blurt out that it *was* true, *all* of it. But he knew he shouldn't.

But before he could speak, Alice said, "Come on, Stu. You don't have to make up stuff in order to have friends. I think you're cool. And I'm sure lots of the other kids will, too, once they know you."

Stu blushed. He felt embarrassed and wished he had never lied in the first place. His uncle had been right.

Everyone was still staring at Stu. Finally Stu looked at Sean's questioning face and said, "My uncle hasn't worked in any movies. He's a baker."

Sean's eyes narrowed. He glared at Stu. "So you lied about everything," he growled. "That's really uncool." Sean was about to say more, but Miss Pender interrupted him.

"That's enough, Sean," Miss Pender said. "Stu admitted that he lied. He just wanted to make friends, that's all."

"Well, it's the wrong way to do it," Sean said, but he wasn't as angry.

"Stu was wrong, but everyone makes mistakes," said Miss Pender as she walked away from the kids.

"Know what I think?" Alice said to Sean and Stu. "You guys are the two biggest monster freaks on Earth! You should be friends!"

Sean looked at Alice and then at Stu and shrugged.

Then Sean smiled and said, "I've got to admit that T-Rex made the day a lot more fun."

"Really?" said Stu.

"Sure," said Sean. "But Stu, you didn't have to lie to fit in."

"You're right," said Stu quickly. "And I'm sorry. All those stories just got away from me."

"Just like the T-Rex almost did!" laughed Alice.

"Well, I'll let it go this time," Sean replied. "The lies I mean, not the T-Rex!"

"Thanks," Stu said. "Why don't we all go to the movies tonight? We can see *Titanoid Versus the Pulsatron*. You, me, and Alice . . . and it will be my treat!" Stu said excitedly.

"Okay, sounds cool," said Sean. "I haven't seen that movie yet."

"And we can stop at my uncle's bakery on the way," Stu added. "He'll give us some of his monster cookies to munch on!"

Stu turned to Alice and asked, "What do you think about going to the movies?"

"I'll go with you both on one condition," she said.

"What's that?" asked Stu and Sean.

Alice pointed at the inflatable dinosaur and said, "T-Rex isn't invited!"